# THE
# SIGN PAINTER'S
# DREAM

PAINTER'S

ROGER ROTH    CROWN PUBLISHERS, INC. · New York

To my dear talented sister, Nita Dossin,
without whose help there'd be no story

To my dear parents, Bernhard and Claire Roth,
without whose help there'd be no me

Copyright © 1993 by Roger Roth.

Published by Crown Publishers, Inc., a Random House company, 225 Park Avenue South,
New York, New York 10003

CROWN is a trademark of Crown Publishers, Inc.
Manufactured in the United States of America

Library of Congress Cataloging-in-Publication Data
Roth, Roger
The sign painter's dream / by Roger Roth.
p.  cm.
Summary:  A spunky old woman's request and a rather unusual dream convince Crabby Clarence the
sign painter to make the most glorious and magnificent sign of his career and then give it away.
[1. Signs and signboards—Fiction.  2. Generosity—Fiction.  3. Dreams—Fiction.]  I. Title.
PZ7.R736Si   1993
[E]—dc20                                                                                          92-13041

ISBN  0-517-58920-6  (trade)
0-517-58921-4  (lib. bdg.)

10 9 8 7 6 5 4 3 2 1

First Edition

Clarence was a sign painter, and Amanda was his cat. For many years, Clarence had been painting signs for people in the little town where he lived.

People called him "Crabby Clarence" because he complained about everything.  He complained about the weather, about the price of paint, even about the price of cat food.  But most of all, he complained about his job.

"This job is so boring!"  Clarence would moan.  "Just look at these boring signs!"

Amanda stood up and rubbed her furry back against one large sign.

"You *like* that sign?  Don't give me a headache!" cried Clarence.  "I painted the very same sign just last week.  It's the same old stuff, day after day after day!"

Amanda yawned widely.

Although Clarence was always in a bad mood, people kept ordering signs because he was very good at his job.  He worked quickly but was careful not to make mistakes.  Business was steady, and people liked his work.  But still Clarence was grouchy.

In fact, the only time the sign painter smiled was when he and
Amanda drove home at the end of the workday. He always
looked forward to reading a book after dinner from his big shelf of
history books. His favorites were about the Revolutionary War.

"Why couldn't we have lived in George Washington's day?" Clarence sighed one evening. "Even ordinary people like me were heroes then! They did glorious and magnificent things and were *never* bored. They changed history. They started a new nation . . ."

Amanda, without meaning to be rude, yawned.

Clarence sighed again, and before long he was fast asleep, dreaming about the glory days of the Revolutionary War . . .

The next day, while Clarence was working, a small gray-haired woman and her little dog entered his shop.

"Hallooo!" she said, and smiled up at Clarence. "I need you to paint me a *big* sign," she announced, looking him directly in the eye.

"Well, that's what I'm here for," Clarence snapped.

"What do you want this sign to say?" he asked.

"APPLES," she declared. "That is, FREE APPLES IF YOU NEED 'EM! And I'd like it glorious and magnificent, so that anyone driving down East Orchard Road will notice it. I grow apples, and when they're ripe, I give them away to anyone who needs them."

Clarence frowned as he wrote down some numbers. "Okay, lady. I can make you a sign for only three hundred dollars."

"Three hundred dollars! *Hee-hee-hee!*" The apple lady laughed pleasantly. "You don't understand. I want you to make it for *free*!"

Clarence's face turned purple.

"FREE?" he boomed. "Why should I do it for *free*? Do I look like Santa Claus?"

The apple lady seemed surprised. "But I give away my beautiful apples for free, don't I? You know what my Aunt Tillie used to say —

*A hero is he who helps people for free.*
*A slimeball, you see, will charge them a fee.*"

Clarence's eyebrows hopped up and down furiously. "If I listened to your crazy Aunt Tillie, I'd be in the poorhouse, starving to death!"

The tiny lady smiled soothingly and said, "Of course, if you *do* make a sign for me, I'll give you a nice slice of my *special* apple pie and a great big glass of milk!"

Clarence made an awful face. He *never* drank milk.

"Sorry, lady," he growled. "I don't have time to make signs for free." And he stomped back to his workroom.

Later that evening, after the dinner dishes were done, Clarence sat down in his big chair to read.

"Free apples? Hah!" he muttered as he stared gloomily at his history book. He was mumbling something about "crazy Aunt Tillie" when he dropped off to sleep.

In his dream, Clarence found himself working hard at a bench by lamplight. Suddenly, he heard the clippety-clop of horses out in the street. The door to his shop swung open and . . .

General George Washington stepped into the room, shaking the snow off his cape and boots. Clarence nearly fell off his chair!

With blazing eyes and a booming voice, Washington spoke directly: "Clarence, I need a sign. *Can you do it*?"

"I g-g-guess so," Clarence stammered. "Wh-wh-what kind of sign do you need?"

"I need a *big* sign that says SEND SHOES TO VALLEY FORGE! My men are desperate. Some of them have to walk in the snow with only rags wrapped around their feet."

Clarence thought fast.  "Okay, General, I can do the sign for only three hundred dollars."

"Three hundred dollars!  Don't give me a headache," said George Washington, wrinkling his eyebrows together.  "I want you to make this sign for *free*."

"For *free*?" Clarence gulped.  "B-b-but . . ."

"But nothing," the general interrupted, raising his arm in a salute.  "Remember what Aunt Tillie used to say —

*Ye olde hero is he who helps people for free.*

*Ye olde scoundrel, you see, doth charge them a fee.*

"This is for your country, Clarence.  Now, just make it glorious and magnificent, and I'll pick it up tomorrow."

"Tomorrow?" gasped Clarence.

"Yes!  There's a war on, son, and we're all in a bit of hasty pudding," said the general, and he whirled his long cape about him as he stomped out the door.

Clarence's book slipped from his lap and crashed to the floor.
The clock said midnight.

"Wow!" Clarence gasped. "I must have been dreaming." He
sat staring for a moment and then suddenly jumped out of the
chair. "C'mon, Amanda," he said. "We're going to the shop!"

All through the night, the sounds of sawing, of hammering, drilling, and sanding, could be heard outside the little sign shop. Clarence hummed and whistled as he worked. For the first time in his life, he actually seemed to be enjoying himself.

The sun had just begun to rise when Clarence announced proudly, "We're finished here, Amanda. Let's take a little ride!"

Clarence's truck bounced along the road that led out of town while Amanda sniffed the fresh morning air. As they came over a hill, Clarence saw a big orchard with trees full of bright, ripening apples. He turned up a long, winding driveway at the edge of the orchard.

"This will be great!" Clarence was surprised to hear himself say.
Choosing a good spot near the road, he parked the truck and set to work.

A little while later, he strode proudly up to the farmhouse, onto the porch, and banged loudly on the door.

"Anybody home?" he called.

"Who's there?" squeaked a voice from inside.

"It's Clarence, ma'am," he called through the door. "I've got something for you."

"My goodness," said the apple lady. She opened the door, walked right around Clarence and down the porch steps. Her little dog marched right behind her.

She stopped at the edge of her lawn and looked.

The apple lady was speechless.  Her little dog didn't even bark, and Amanda hopped onto the hood of the truck so that she, too, could gaze at the wonderful sign.

Finally, the apple lady turned to Clarence and said, "You did it. And you remembered to make it glorious and magnificent, too."  She laughed.  "Well, Clarence, now you're a real hero, and you deserve a reward.  Come into the kitchen," she said, waving him in.

As he sat down at the kitchen table, Clarence felt terrific. The sign was the most beautiful he had ever made. He was glad the apple lady liked it so much. And when she set down the most perfect slice of apple pie Clarence had ever seen, along with a tall glass of cold milk, he had never been happier. He even drank *all* the milk, and Clarence *never* drank milk.

From that day on, people stopped calling him "Crabby Clarence." They admired the apple lady's sign and brought Clarence many orders for other glorious and magnificent signs. And now and then, he'd make one just for fun — *and* for free.

In the evening, Clarence still loved to read his history books. But no matter how busy he was, he always found time to help the apple lady pick her apples and give them away to anyone who needed them.

5